Bayard Taylor (January 11, 1825 – December 19, 1878) was an American poet, literary critic, translator, travel author, and diplomat. Taylor was born on January 11, 1825, in Kennett Square in Chester County, Pennsylvania. He was the fourth son, the first to survive to maturity, of the Quaker couple, Joseph and Rebecca (née Way) Taylor. His father was a wealthy farmer. Bayard received his early instruction in an academy at West Chester, Pennsylvania, and later at nearby Unionville. At the age of seventeen, he was apprenticed to a printer in West Chester. The influential critic and editor Rufus Wilmot Griswold encouraged him to write poetry. The volume that resulted, Ximena, or the Battle of the Sierra Morena, and other Poems, was published in 1844 and dedicated to Griswold. Using the money from his poetry and an advance for travel articles, he visited parts of England, France, Germany and Italy, making largely pedestrian tours for almost two years. He sent accounts of his travels to the Tribune, The Saturday Evening Post, and The United States Gazette. (Source: Wikipedia)

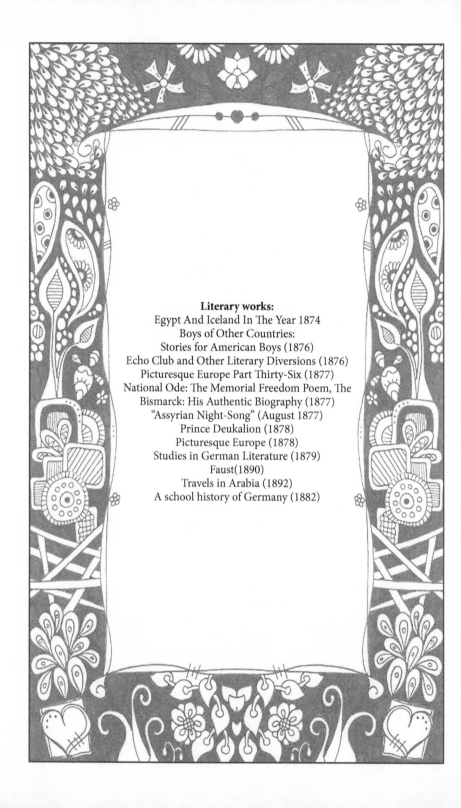

Literary works:
Egypt And Iceland In The Year 1874
Boys of Other Countries:
Stories for American Boys (1876)
Echo Club and Other Literary Diversions (1876)
Picturesque Europe Part Thirty-Six (1877)
National Ode: The Memorial Freedom Poem, The
Bismarck: His Authentic Biography (1877)
"Assyrian Night-Song" (August 1877)
Prince Deukalion (1878)
Picturesque Europe (1878)
Studies in German Literature (1879)
Faust(1890)
Travels in Arabia (1892)
A school history of Germany (1882)

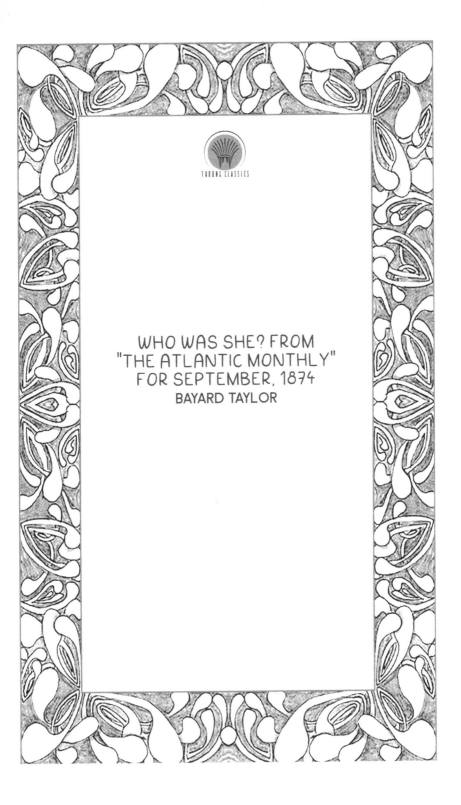

THRONG CLASSICS

WHO WAS SHE? FROM "THE ATLANTIC MONTHLY" FOR SEPTEMBER, 1874

BAYARD TAYLOR

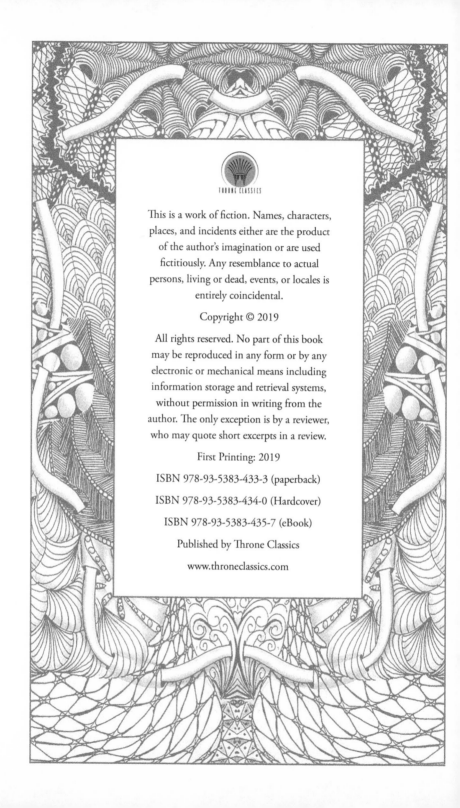

Copyright © 2019

First Printing: 2019

ISBN 978-93-5383-433-3 (paperback)

ISBN 978-93-5383-434-0 (Hardcover)

ISBN 978-93-5383-435-7 (eBook)

Published by Throne Classics

www.throneclassics.com

Contents

WHO WAS SHE? FROM
"THE ATLANTIC MONTHLY"
FOR SEPTEMBER, 1874

WHO WAS SHE?

From "The Atlantic Monthly" for September, 1874

Come, now, there may as well be an end of this! Every time I meet your eyes squarely, I detect the question just slipping out of them. If you had spoken it, or even boldly looked it; if you had shown in your motions the least sign of a fussy or fidgety concern on my account; if this were not the evening of my birthday, and you the only friend who remembered it; if confession were not good for the soul, though harder than sin to some people, of whom I am one—well, if all reasons were not at this instant converged into a focus, and burning me rather violently, in that region where the seat of emotion is supposed to lie, I should keep my trouble to myself.

Yes, I have fifty times had it on my mind to tell you the whole story. But who can be certain that his best friend will not smile—or, what is worse, cherish a kind of charitable pity ever afterward—when the external forms of a very serious kind of passion seem trivial, fantastic, foolish? And the worst of all is that the heroic part which I imagined I was playing proves to have been almost the reverse. The only comfort which I can find in my humiliation is that I am capable of feeling it. There isn't a bit of a paradox in this, as you will see; but I only mention it, now, to prepare you for, maybe, a little morbid sensitiveness of my moral nerves.

The documents are all in this portfolio under my elbow. I had just read them again completely through when you were announced. You may examine them as you like afterward: for the present, fill your glass, take another Cabana, and keep silent until my "ghastly tale" has reached its most lamentable conclusion.

The beginning of it was at Wampsocket Springs, three years ago last summer. I suppose most unmarried men who have reached, or passed, the age of thirty—and I was then thirty-three—experience a milder return of their adolescent warmth, a kind of fainter second spring, since the first has not fulfilled its promise. Of course, I wasn't clearly conscious of this at the time:

who is? But I had had my youthful passion and my tragic disappointment, as you know: I had looked far enough into what Thackeray used to call the cryptic mysteries to save me from the Scylla of dissipation, and yet preserved enough of natural nature to keep me out of the Pharisaic Charybdis. My devotion to my legal studies had already brought me a mild distinction; the paternal legacy was a good nest-egg for the incubation of wealth—in short, I was a fair, respectable "party," desirable to the humbler mammas, and not to be despised by the haughty exclusives.

The fashionable hotel at the Springs holds three hundred, and it was packed. I had meant to lounge there for a fortnight and then finish my holidays at Long Branch; but eighty, at least, out of the three hundred were young and moved lightly in muslin. With my years and experience I felt so safe that to walk, talk, or dance with them became simply a luxury, such as I had never— at least so freely—possessed before. My name and standing, known to some families, were agreeably exaggerated to the others, and I enjoyed that supreme satisfaction which a man always feels when he discovers, or imagines, that he is popular in society. There is a kind of premonitory apology implied in my saying this, I am aware. You must remember that I am culprit, and culprit's counsel, at the same time.

You have never been at Wampsocket? Well, the hills sweep around in a crescent, on the northern side, and four or five radiating glens, descending from them, unite just above the village. The central one, leading to a waterfall (called "Minne-hehe" by the irreverent young people, because there is so little of it), is the fashionable drive and promenade; but the second ravine on the left, steep, crooked, and cumbered with bowlders which have tumbled from somewhere and lodged in the most extraordinary groupings, became my favorite walk of a morning. There was a footpath in it, well-trodden at first, but gradually fading out as it became more like a ladder than a path, and I soon discovered that no other city feet than mine were likely to scale a certain rough slope which seemed the end of the ravine. With the aid of the tough laurel-stems I climbed to the top, passed through a cleft as narrow as a doorway, and presently found myself in a little upper dell, as wild and sweet and strange as one of the pictures that haunts us on the brink of sleep.

There was a pond—no, rather a bowl—of water in the centre; hardly twenty yards across, yet the sky in it was so pure and far down that the circle of rocks and summer foliage inclosing it seemed like a little planetary ring, floating off alone through space. I can't explain the charm of the spot, nor the selfishness which instantly suggested that I should keep the discovery to myself. Ten years earlier I should have looked around for some fair spirit to be my "minister," but now—

One forenoon—I think it was the third or fourth time I had visited the place—I was startled to find the dent of a heel in the earth, half-way up the slope. There had been rain during the night and the earth was still moist and soft. It was the mark of a woman's boot, only to be distinguished from that of a walking-stick by its semicircular form. A little higher, I found the outline of a foot, not so small as to awake an ecstasy, but with a suggestion of lightness, elasticity, and grace. If hands were thrust through holes in a board-fence, and nothing of the attached bodies seen, I can easily imagine that some would attract and others repel us: with footprints the impression is weaker, of course, but we cannot escape it. I am not sure whether I wanted to find the unknown wearer of the boot within my precious personal solitude: I was afraid I should see her, while passing through the rocky crevice, and yet was disappointed when I found no one.

But on the flat, warm rock overhanging the tarn—my special throne—lay some withering wild-flowers and a book! I looked up and down, right and left: there was not the slightest sign of another human life than mine. Then I lay down for a quarter of an hour, and listened: there were only the noises of bird and squirrel, as before. At last, I took up the book, the flat breadth of which suggested only sketches. There were, indeed, some tolerable studies of rocks and trees on the first pages; a few not very striking caricatures, which seemed to have been commenced as portraits, but recalled no faces I knew; then a number of fragmentary notes, written in pencil. I found no name, from first to last; only, under the sketches, a monogram so complicated and laborious that the initials could hardly be discovered unless one already knew them.

The writing was a woman's, but it had surely taken its character from

11

certain features of her own: it was clear, firm, individual. It had nothing of that air of general debility which usually marks the manuscript of young ladies, yet its firmness was far removed from the stiff, conventional slope which all Englishwomen seem to acquire in youth and retain through life, I don't see how any man in my situation could have helped reading a few lines—if only for the sake of restoring lost property. But I was drawn on and on, and finished by reading all: thence, since no further harm could be done, I reread, pondering over certain passages until they stayed with me. Here they are, as I set them down, that evening, on the back of a legal blank:

"It makes a great deal of difference whether we wear social forms as bracelets or handcuffs."

"Can we not still be wholly our independent selves, even while doing, in the main, as others do? I know two who are so; but they are married."

"The men who admire these bold, dashing young girls treat them like weaker copies of themselves. And yet they boast of what they call 'experience'!"

"I wonder if any one felt the exquisite beauty of the noon as I did to-day? A faint appreciation of sunsets and storms is taught us in youth, and kept alive by novels and flirtations; but the broad, imperial splendor of this summer noon!—and myself standing alone in it—yes, utterly alone!" "The men I seek must exist: where are they? How make an acquaintance, when one obsequiously bows himself away, as I advance? The fault is surely not all on my side."

There was much more, intimate enough to inspire me with a keen interest in the writer, yet not sufficiently so to make my perusal a painful indiscretion. I yielded to the impulse of the moment, took out my pencil, and wrote a dozen lines on one of the blank pages. They ran something in this wise:

"*IGNOTUS IGNOTÆ!—You have bestowed without intending it,*

and I have taken without your knowledge. Do not regret the

accident which has enriched another. This concealed idyl of

the hills was mine, as I supposed, but I acknowledge your

equal right to it. Shall we share the possession, or will

you banish me?"

There was a frank advance, tempered by a proper caution, I fancied, in the words I wrote. It was evident that she was unmarried, but outside of that certainty there lay a vast range of possibilities, some of them alarming enough. However, if any nearer acquaintance should arise out of the incident, the next step must be taken by her. Was I one of the men she sought? I almost imagined so—certainly hoped so.

I laid the book on the rock, as I had found it, bestowed another keen scrutiny on the lonely landscape, and then descended the ravine. That evening, I went early to the ladies' parlor, chatted more than usual with the various damsels whom I knew, and watched with a new interest those whom I knew not. My mind, involuntarily, had already created a picture of the unknown. She might be twenty-five, I thought; a reflective habit of mind would hardly be developed before that age. Tall and stately, of course; distinctly proud in her bearing, and somewhat reserved in her manners. Why she should have large dark eyes, with long dark lashes, I could not tell; but so I seemed to see her. Quite forgetting that I was (or had meant to be) Ignotus, I found myself staring rather significantly at one or the other of the young ladies, in whom I discovered some slight general resemblance to the imaginary character. My fancies, I must confess, played strange pranks with me. They had been kept

13

in a coop so many years that now, when I suddenly turned them loose, their rickety attempts at flight quite bewildered me.

No! there was no use in expecting a sudden discovery. I went to the glen betimes, next morning: the book was gone and so were the faded flowers, but some of the latter were scattered over the top of another rock, a few yards from mine. Ha! this means that I am not to withdraw, I said to myself: she makes room for me! But how to surprise her?—for by this time I was fully resolved to make her acquaintance, even though she might turn out to be forty, scraggy, and sandy-haired.

I knew no other way so likely as that of visiting the glen at all times of the day. I even went so far as to write a line of greeting, with a regret that our visits had not yet coincided, and laid it under a stone on the top of her rock. The note disappeared, but there was no answer in its place. Then I suddenly remembered her fondness for the noon hours, at which time she was "utterly alone." The hotel table d'hôte was at one o'clock: her family, doubtless, dined later, in their own rooms. Why, this gave me, at least, her place in society! The question of age, to be sure, remained unsettled; but all else was safe.

The next day I took a late and large breakfast, and sacrificed my dinner. Before noon the guests had all straggled back to the hotel from glen and grove and lane, so bright and hot was the sunshine. Indeed, I could hardly have supported the reverberation of heat from the sides of the ravine but for a fixed belief that I should be successful. While crossing the narrow meadow upon which it opened, I caught a glimpse of something white among the thickets higher up. A moment later it had vanished, and I quickened my pace, feeling the beginning of an absurd nervous excitement in my limbs. At the next turn, there it was again! but only for another moment. I paused, exulting, and wiped my drenched forehead. "She cannot escape me!" I murmured between the deep draughts of cooler air I inhaled in the shadow of a rock.

A few hundred steps more brought me to the foot of the steep ascent, where I had counted on overtaking her. I was too late for that, but the dry, baked soil had surely been crumbled and dislodged, here and there, by a rapid foot. I followed, in reckless haste, snatching at the laurel branches right and left, and paying little heed to my footing. About, one-third of the way up I slipped, fell, caught a bush which snapped at the root, slid, whirled over, and before I fairly knew what had happened, I was lying doubled up at the bottom of the slope.

I rose, made two steps forward, and then sat down with a groan of pain; my left ankle was badly sprained, in addition to various minor scratches and bruises. There was a revulsion of feeling, of course—instant, complete, and hideous. I fairly hated the Unknown. "Fool that I was!" I exclaimed, in the theatrical manner, dashing the palm of my hand softly against my brow: "lured to this by the fair traitress! But, no!—not fair: she shows the artfulness of faded, desperate spinsterhood; she is all compact of enamel, 'liquid bloom of youth' and hair dye!"

There was a fierce comfort in this thought, but it couldn't help me out of the scrape. I dared not sit still, lest a sunstroke should be added, and there was no resource but to hop or crawl down the rugged path, in the hope of finding a forked sapling from which I could extemporize a crutch. With endless pain and trouble I reached a thicket, and was feebly working on a branch with my pen-knife, when the sound of a heavy footstep surprised me.

A brown harvest-hand, in straw hat and shirtsleeves, presently appeared. He grinned when he saw me, and the thick snub of his nose would have seemed like a sneer at any other time.

"Are you the gentleman that got hurt?" he asked. "Is it pretty tolerable bad?"

"Who said I was hurt?" I cried, in astonishment.

"One of your town-women from the hotel—I reckon she was. I was binding oats, in the field over the ridge; but I haven't lost no time in comin' here."

While I was stupidly staring at this announcement, he whipped out a big clasp-knife, and in a few minutes fashioned me a practicable crutch. Then, taking me by the other arm, he set me in motion toward the village.

Grateful as I was for the man's help, he aggravated me by his ignorance.

When I asked if he knew the lady, he answered: "It's more'n likely you know her better," But where did she come from? Down from the hill, he guessed, but it might ha' been up the road. How did she look? was she old or young? what was the color of her eyes? of her hair? There, now, I was too much for him. When a woman kept one o' them speckled veils over her face, turned her head away, and held her parasol between, how were you to know her from Adam? I declare to you, I couldn't arrive at one positive particular. Even when he affirmed that she was tall, he added, the next instant: "Now I come to think on it, she stepped mighty quick; so I guess she must ha' been short."

By the time we reached the hotel, I was in a state of fever; opiates and lotions had their will of me for the rest of the day. I was glad to escape the worry of questions, and the conventional sympathy expressed in inflections of the voice which are meant to soothe, and only exasperate. The next morning, as I lay upon my sofa, restful, patient, and properly cheerful, the waiter entered with a bouquet of wild flowers.

"Who sent them?" I asked.

"I found them outside your door, sir. Maybe there's a card; yes, here's a bit o' paper."

I opened the twisted slip he handed me, and read: "From your dell—and mine." I took the flowers; among them were two or three rare and beautiful varieties which I had only found in that one spot. Fool, again! I noiselessly kissed, while pretending to smell them, had them placed on a stand within reach, and fell into a state of quiet and agreeable contemplation.

Tell me, yourself, whether any male human being is ever too old for sentiment, provided that it strikes him at the right time and in the right way! What did that bunch of wild flowers betoken? Knowledge, first; then, sympathy; and finally, encouragement, at least. Of course she had seen my accident, from above; of course she had sent the harvest laborer to aid me home. It was quite natural she should imagine some special, romantic interest in the lonely dell, on my part, and the gift took additional value from her conjecture.

Four days afterward, there was a hop in the large dining-room of the hotel. Early in the morning, a fresh bouquet had been left at my door. I was tired of my enforced idleness, eager to discover the fair unknown (she was again fair, to my fancy!), and I determined to go down, believing that a cane and a crimson velvet slipper on the left foot would provoke a glance of sympathy from certain eyes, and thus enable me to detect them.

The fact was, the sympathy was much too general and effusive. Everybody, it seemed, came to me with kindly greetings; seats were vacated at my approach, even fat Mrs. Huxter insisting on my taking her warm place, at the head of the room. But Bob Leroy—you know him—as gallant a gentleman as ever lived, put me down at the right point, and kept me there. He only meant to divert me, yet gave me the only place where I could quietly inspect all the younger ladies, as dance or supper brought them near.

One of the dances was an old-fashioned cotillon, and one of the figures, the "coquette," brought every one, in turn, before me. I received a pleasant word or two from those whom I knew, and a long, kind, silent glance from Miss May Danvers. Where had been my eyes? She was tall, stately, twenty-five, had large dark eyes, and long dark lashes! Again the changes of the dance brought her near me; I threw (or strove to throw) unutterable meanings into my eyes, and cast them upon hers. She seemed startled, looked suddenly away, looked back to me, and—blushed. I knew her for what is called "a nice girl"— that is, tolerably frank, gently feminine, and not dangerously intelligent. Was it possible that I had overlooked so much character and intellect?

As the cotillon closed, she was again in my neighborhood, and her partner led her in my direction. I was rising painfully from my chair, when Bob Leroy pushed me down again, whisked another seat from somewhere, planted it at my side, and there she was!

She knew who was her neighbor, I plainly saw; but instead of turning toward me, she began to fan herself in a nervous way and to fidget with the buttons of her gloves. I grew impatient.

"Miss Danvers!" I said, at last.

"Oh!" was all her answer, as she looked at me for a moment.

"Where are your thoughts?" I asked.

Then she turned, with wide, astonished eyes, coloring softly up to the roots of her hair. My heart gave a sudden leap.

"How can you tell, if I can not?" she asked.

"May I guess?"

She made a slight inclination of the head, saying nothing. I was then quite sure.

"The second ravine to the left of the main drive?"

This time she actually started; her color became deeper, and a leaf of the ivory fan snapped between her fingers.

"Let there be no more a secret!" I exclaimed. "Your flowers have brought me your messages; I knew I should find you—"

Full of certainty, I was speaking in a low, impassioned voice. She cut me short by rising from her seat; I felt that she was both angry and alarmed. Fisher, of Philadelphia, jostling right and left in his haste, made his way toward her. She fairly snatched his arm, clung to it with a warmth I had never seen expressed in a ballroom, and began to whisper in his ear. It was not five minutes before he came to me, alone, with a very stern face, bent down, and said:

"If you have discovered our secret, you will keep silent. You are certainly a gentleman."

I bowed, coldly and savagely. There was a draught from the open window; my ankle became suddenly weary and painful, and I went to bed. Can you believe that I didn't guess, immediately, what it all meant? In a vague way, I fancied that I had been premature in my attempt to drop our mutual incognito, and that Fisher, a rival lover, was jealous of me. This was rather flattering than otherwise; but when I limped down to the ladies' parlor, the next day, no Miss Danvers was to be seen. I did not venture to ask for her; it might seem importunate, and a woman of so much hidden capacity was evidently not to be wooed in the ordinary way.

So another night passed by; and then, with the morning, came a letter which made me feel, at the same instant, like a fool and a hero. It had been dropped in the Wampsocket post-office, was legibly addressed to me and delivered with some other letters which had arrived by the night mail. Here it is; listen:

"*Noto Ignota!*—*Haste is not a gift of the gods, and you have been impatient, with the usual result. I was almost prepared for this, and thus am not wholly disappointed. In a day or two more you will discover your mistake, which, so far as I can learn, has done no particular harm. If you wish to find me, there is only one way to seek me; should I tell you what it is, I should run the risk of losing you—that is, I should preclude the manifestation of a certain quality which I hope to find in the man who may—or—, rather, must—be my friend. This sounds enigmatical, yet you have read enough of my nature, as written in those random notes in my sketch-book, to guess, at least, how much I require. Only this let me add: mere guessing is useless.*

"*Being unknown, I can write freely. If you find me, I shall be justified; if not, I shall hardly need to blush, even to myself, over a futile experiment.*

"*It is possible for me to learn enough of your life, henceforth, to direct my relation toward you. This may be the end; if so, I shall know it soon. I shall also know*

whether you continue to seek me. Trusting in your honor as a

man, I must ask you to trust in mine, as a woman."

I did discover my mistake, as the Unknown promised. There had been a secret betrothal between Fisher and Miss Danvers, and, singularly enough, the momentous question and answer had been given in the very ravine leading to my upper dell! The two meant to keep the matter to themselves; but therein, it seems, I thwarted them; there was a little opposition on the part of their respective families, but all was amicably settled before I left Wampsocket.

The letter made a very deep impression upon me. What was the one way to find her? What could it be but the triumph that follows ambitious toil—the manifestation of all my best qualities as a man? Be she old or young, plain or beautiful, I reflected, hers is surely a nature worth knowing, and its candid intelligence conceals no hazards for me. I have sought her rashly, blundered, betrayed that I set her lower, in my thoughts, than her actual self: let me now adopt the opposite course, seek her openly no longer, go back to my tasks, and, following my own aims vigorously and cheerfully, restore that respect which she seemed to be on the point of losing. For, consciously or not, she had communicated to me a doubt, implied in the very expression of her own strength and pride. She had meant to address me as an equal, yet, despite herself, took a stand a little above that which she accorded to me.

I came back to New York earlier than usual, worked steadily at my profession and with increasing success, and began to accept opportunities (which I had previously declined) of making myself personally known to the great, impressible, fickle, tyrannical public. One or two of my speeches in the hall of the Cooper Institute, on various occasions—as you may perhaps remember—gave me a good headway with the party, and were the chief cause of my nomination for the State office which I still hold. (There, on the table, lies a resignation, written to-day, but not yet signed. We'll talk of it afterward.) Several months passed by, and no further letter reached me. I gave up much of my time to society, moved familiarly in more than one province of the kingdom here, and vastly extended my acquaintance, especially among the women; but not one of them betrayed the mysterious something or other—really I can't explain precisely what it was!—which I was looking for. In fact, the more I endeavored quietly to study the sex, the more confused I became.

At last, I was subjected to the usual onslaught from the strong-minded. A small but formidable committee entered my office one morning and demanded a categorical declaration of my principles. What my views on the subject were, I knew very well; they were clear and decided; and yet, I hesitated to declare them! It wasn't a temptation of Saint Anthony—that is, turned the other way—and the belligerent attitude of the dames did not alarm me in the least; but she! What was her position? How could I best please her? It flashed upon my mind, while Mrs. ———— was making her formal speech that I had taken no step for months without a vague, secret reference to her. So I strove to be courteous, friendly, and agreeably noncommittal; begged for further documents, and promised to reply by letter in a few days.

I was hardly surprised to find the well-known hand on the envelope of a letter shortly afterward. I held it for a minute in my palm, with an absurd hope that I might sympathetically feel its character before breaking the seal. Then I read it with a great sense of relief.

"I have never assumed to guide a man, except toward the full

exercise of his powers. It is not opinion in action, but

opinion in a state of idleness or indifference, which repels

me. I am deeply glad that you have gained so much since you

left the country. If, in shaping your course, you have

thought of me, I will frankly say that, to that extent,

you have drawn nearer. Am I mistaken in conjecturing that

you wish to know my relation to the movement concerning

which you were recently interrogated? In this, as in other

instances which may come, I must beg you to consider me only

21

as a spectator. The more my own views may seem likely to

sway your action, the less I shall be inclined to declare

them. If you find this cold or unwomanly, remember that it

is not easy!"

Yes! I felt that I had certainly drawn much nearer to her. And from this time on, her imaginary face and form became other than they were. She was twenty-eight—three years older; a very little above the middle height, but not tall; serene, rather than stately, in her movements; with a calm, almost grave face, relieved by the sweetness of the full, firm lips; and finally eyes of pure, limpid gray, such as we fancy-belonged to the Venus of Milo. I found her thus much more attractive than with the dark eyes and lashes—but she did not make her appearance in the circles which I frequented.

Another year slipped away. As an official personage, my importance increased, but I was careful not to exaggerate it to myself. Many have wondered (perhaps you among the rest) at my success, seeing that I possess no remarkable abilities. If I have any secret, it is simply this—doing faithfully, with all my might, whatever I undertake. Nine-tenths of our politicians become inflated and careless, after the first few years, and are easily forgotten when they once lose place.

I am a little surprised now that I had so much patience with the Unknown. I was too important, at least, to be played with; too mature to be! subjected to a longer test; too earnest, as I had proved, to be doubted, or thrown aside without a further explanation.

Growing tired, at last, of silent waiting, I bethought me of advertising. A carefully written "Personal," in which Ignotus informed Ignota of the necessity of his communicating with her, appeared simultaneously in the "Tribune," "Herald," "World," and "Times." I renewed the advertisement as the time expired without an answer, and I think it was about the end of the third week before one came, through the post, as before.

Ah, yes! I had forgotten. See! my advertisement is pasted on the note, as a heading or motto for the manuscript lines. I don't know why the printed slip should give me a particular feeling of humiliation as I look at it, but such is the fact. What she wrote is all I need read to you:

"I could not, at first, be certain that this was meant for

me. If I were to explain to you why I have not written for

so long a time, I might give you one of the few clews which

I insist on keeping in my own hands. In your public

capacity, you have been (so far as a woman may judge)

upright, independent, wholly manly in your relations with

other men I learn nothing of you that is not honorables

toward women you are kind, chivalrous, no doubt, overflowing

with the usual social refinements, but—Here, again, I

run hard upon the absolute necessity of silence. The way to

me, if you care to traverse it, is so simple, so very simple!

Yet, after what I have written, I can not even wave my

hand in the direction of it, without certain self-contempt.

When I feel free to tell you, we shall draw apart and remain

unknown forever.

"You desire to write? I do not prohibit it. I have

heretofore made no arrangement for hearing from you, in

turn, because I could not discover that any advantage would

accrue from it. But it seems only fair, I confess, and you

dare not think me capricious. So, three days hence, at six

o'clock in the evening, a trusty messenger of mine will call at your door. If you have anything to give her for me, the

act of giving it must be the sign of a compact on your part

that you will allow her to leave immediately, unquestioned

and unfollowed."

You look puzzled, I see: you don't catch the real drift of her words? Well, that's a melancholy encouragement. Neither did I, at the time: it was plain that I had disappointed her in some way, and my intercourse with or manner toward women had something to do with it. In vain I ran over as much of my later social life as I could recall. There had been no special attention, nothing to mislead a susceptible heart; on the other side, certainly no rudeness, no want of "chivalrous" (she used the word!) respect and attention. What, in the name of all the gods, was the matter?

In spite of all my efforts to grow clearer, I was obliged to write my letter in a rather muddled state of mind. I had so much to say! sixteen folio pages, I was sure, would only suffice for an introduction to the case; yet, when the creamy vellum lay before me and the moist pen drew my fingers toward it, I sat stock dumb for half an hour. I wrote, finally, in a half-desperate mood, without regard to coherency or logic. Here's a rough draft of a part of the letter, and a single passage from it will be enough:

I can conceive of no simpler way to you than the knowledge

of your name and address. I have drawn airy images of you,

but they do not become incarnate, and I am not sure that I

should recognize you in the brief moment of passing. Your

nature is not of those which are instantly legible. As an

abstract power, it has wrought in my life and it continually

moves my heart with desires which are unsatisfactory because

so vague and ignorant. Let me offer you, personally, my

gratitude, my earnest friendship: you would laugh if I were now to offer more.

Stay! here is another fragment, more reckless in tone:

"I want to find the woman whom I can love—who can love me.

But this is a masquerade where the features are hidden, the

voice disguised, even the hands grotesquely gloved. Come! I

will venture more than I ever thought was possible to me.

You shall know my deepest nature as I myself seem to know

it. Then, give me the commonest chance of learning yours,

through an intercourse which shall leave both free, should

we not feel the closing of the inevitable bond!"

After I had written that, the pages filled rapidly. When the appointed hour arrived, a bulky epistle, in a strong linen envelope, sealed with five wax seals, was waiting on my table. Precisely at six there was an announcement: the door opened, and a little outside, in the shadow, I saw an old woman, in a threadbare dress of rusty black.

"Come in!" I said.

"The letter!" answered a husky voice. She stretched out a bony hand, without moving a step.

"It is for a lady—very important business," said I, taking up the letter; "are you sure that there is no mistake?"

She drew her hand under the shawl, turned without a word, and moved toward the hall door.

"Stop!" I cried: "I beg a thousand pardons! Take it—take it! You are the right messenger!"

She clutched it, and was instantly gone.

Several days passed, and I gradually became so nervous and uneasy that

I was on the point of inserting another "Personal" in the daily papers, when the answer arrived. It was brief and mysterious; you shall hear the whole of it:

"I thank you. Your letter is a sacred confidence which I

pray you never to regret. Your nature is sound and good. You

ask no more than is reasonable, and I have no real right to

refuse. In the one respect which I have hinted, I may have

been unskilful or too narrowly cautious: I must have the

certainty of this. Therefore, as a generous favor, give me

six months more! At the end of that time I will write to you

again. Have patience with these brief lines: another word

might be a word too much."

You notice the change in her tone? The letter gave me the strongest impression of a new, warm, almost anxious interest on her part. My fancies, as first at Wampsocket, began to play all sorts of singular pranks: sometimes she was rich and of an old family, sometimes moderately poor and obscure, but always the same calm, reposeful face and clear gray eyes. I ceased looking for her in society, quite sure that I should not find her, and nursed a wild expectation of suddenly meeting her, face to face, in the most unlikely places and under startling circumstances. However, the end of it all was patience—patience for six months.

There's not much more to tell; but this last letter is hard for me to read. It came punctually, to a day. I knew it would, and at the last I began to dread the time, as if a heavy note were falling due, and I had no funds to meet it. My head was in a whirl when I broke the seal. The fact in it stared at me blankly, at once, but it was a long time before the words and sentences became intelligible.

"The stipulated time has come, and our hidden romance is at

an end. Had I taken this resolution a year ago, it would

have saved me many vain hopes, and you, perhaps, a little uncertainty. Forgive me, first, if you can, and then hear the explanation!

"You wished for a personal interview: you have had, not one, but many. We have met, in society, talked face to face, discussed the weather, the opera, toilettes, Queechy, Aurora Floyd, Long Branch, and Newport, and exchanged a weary amount of fashionable gossip; and you never guessed that I was governed by any deeper interest! I have purposely uttered ridiculous platitudes, and you were as smilingly courteous as if you enjoyed them: I have let fall remarks whose hollowness and selfishness could not have escaped you, and have waited in vain for a word of sharp, honest, manly reproof. Your manner to me was unexceptionable, as it was to all other women: but there lies the source of my disappointment, of—yes—of my sorrow!

"You appreciate, I can not doubt, the qualities in woman which men value in one another—culture, independence of thought, a high and earnest apprehension of life; but you know not how to seek them. It is not true that a mature and unperverted woman is flattered by receiving only the general obsequiousness which most men give to the whole sex. In the man who contradicts and strives with her, she discovers a

27

truer interest, a nobler respect. The empty-headed, spindle-

shanked youths who dance admirably, understand something of

billiards, much less of horses, and still less of

navigation, soon grow inexpressibly wearisome to us; but the

men who adopt their social courtesy, never seeking to

arouse, uplift, instruct us, are a bitter disappointment.

"What would have been the end, had you really found me?
Certainly a sincere, satisfying friendship. No mysterious

magnetic force has drawn you to me or held you near me, nor

has my experiment inspired me with an interest which can not

be given up without a personal pang. I am grieved, for the

sake of all men and all women. Yet, understand me! I mean no

slightest reproach. I esteem and honor you for what you

are. Farewell!"

There! Nothing could be kinder in tone, nothing more humiliating in substance, I was sore and offended for a few days; but I soon began to see, and ever more and more clearly, that she was wholly right. I was sure, also, that any further attempt to correspond with her would be vain. It all comes of taking society just as we find it, and supposing that conventional courtesy is the only safe ground on which men and women can meet.

The fact is—there's no use in hiding it from myself (and I see, by your face, that the letter cuts into your own conscience)—she is a free, courageous, independent character, and—I am not. But who was she?

About Author

Life and work

Taylor was born on January 11, 1825, in Kennett Square in Chester County, Pennsylvania. He was the fourth son, the first to survive to maturity, of the Quaker couple, Joseph and Rebecca (née Way) Taylor. His father was a wealthy farmer. Bayard received his early instruction in an academy at West Chester, Pennsylvania, and later at nearby Unionville. At the age of seventeen, he was apprenticed to a printer in West Chester. The influential critic and editor Rufus Wilmot Griswold encouraged him to write poetry. The volume that resulted, Ximena, or the Battle of the Sierra Morena, and other Poems, was published in 1844 and dedicated to Griswold.

Using the money from his poetry and an advance for travel articles, he visited parts of England, France, Germany and Italy, making largely pedestrian tours for almost two years. He sent accounts of his travels to the Tribune, The Saturday Evening Post, and The United States Gazette.

In 1846, he published a collection of those articles in two volumes as Views Afoot, or Europe seen with Knapsack and Staff. That publication resulted in an invitation to serve as an editorial assistant for Graham's Magazine for a few months in 1848. That same year, Horace Greeley, editor of the New York Tribune, hired Taylor and sent him to California to report on the gold rush. He returned by way of Mexico and published another two-volume collection of travel essays, El Dorado; or, Adventures in the Path of Empire (1850). Within two weeks of release, the books sold 10,000 copies in the U.S. and 30,000 in Great Britain.

In 1849 Taylor married Mary Agnew, who died of tuberculosis the next year. That same year, Taylor won a popular competition sponsored by P. T. Barnum to write an ode for the "Swedish Nightingale", singer Jenny Lind. His poem "Greetings to America" was set to music by Julius Benedict and performed by the singer at numerous concerts on her tour of the United States.

In 1851 he traveled to Egypt, where he followed the Nile River as far as 12° 30' N. He also traveled in Palestine and Mediterranean countries, writing poetry based on his experiences. Toward the end of 1852, he sailed from England to Calcutta, and then to China, where he joined the expedition of Commodore Matthew Calbraith Perry to Japan. The results of these journeys were published as A Journey to Central Africa; or, Life and Landscapes from Egypt to the Negro Kingdoms of the White Nile (1854); The Lands of the Saracen; or, Pictures of Palestine, Asia Minor, Sicily and Spain (1854); and A Visit to India, China and Japan in the Year 1853 (1855).

He returned to the U.S. on December 20, 1853, and undertook a successful public lecturer tour that extended from Maine to Wisconsin. After two years, he went to northern Europe to study Swedish life, language and literature. The trip inspired his long narrative poem Lars. His series of articles Swedish Letters to the Tribune were republished as Northern Travel: Summer and Winter Pictures (1857).

In Berlin in 1856, Taylor met the great German scientist Alexander von Humboldt, hoping to interview him for the New York Tribune. Humboldt was welcoming, and inquired whether they should speak English or German. Taylor planned to go to central Asia, where Humboldt had traveled in 1829. Taylor informed Humboldt of Washington Irving's death; Humboldt had met him in Paris. Taylor saw Humboldt again in 1857 at Potsdam.

In October 1857, he married Maria Hansen, the daughter of the Danish/German astronomer Peter Hansen. The couple spent the following winter in Greece. In 1859 Taylor returned to the American West and lectured at San Francisco.

In 1862, he was appointed to the U.S. diplomatic service as secretary of legation at St. Petersburg, and acting minister to Russia for a time during 1862-3 after the resignation of Ambassador Simon Cameron.

He published his first novel Hannah Thurston in 1863. The newspaper The New York Times first praised him for "break[ing] new ground with such assured success". A second much longer appreciation in the same newspaper was thoroughly negative, describing "one pointless, aimless situation leading to another of the same stamp, and so on in maddening succession". It concluded: "The platitudes and puerilities which might otherwise only raise a smile, when confronted with such pompous pretensions, excite the contempt of every man who has in him the feeblest instincts of common honesty in literature." It proved successful enough for his publisher to announce another novel from him the next year.

In 1864 Taylor and his wife Maria returned to the U.S. In 1866, Taylor traveled to Colorado and made a large loop through the northern mountains on horseback with a group that included William Byers, editor of the newspaper Rocky Mountain News. His letters describing this adventure were later compiled and published as Colorado: A Summer Trip.

His late novel, Joseph and His Friend: A Story of Pennsylvania (1870), first serialized in the magazine The Atlantic, was described as a story of young man in rural Pennsylvania and "the troubles which arise from the want of a broader education and higher culture". It is believed to be based on the poets Fitz-Greene Halleck and Joseph Rodman Drake, and since the late 20th-century has been called America's first gay novel. Taylor spoke at the dedication of a monument to Halleck in his native town, Guilford, Connecticut. He said that in establishing this monument to an American poet "we symbolize the intellectual growth of the American people.... The life of the poet who sleeps here represents the long period of transition between the appearance of American poetry and the creation of an appreciative and sympathetic audience for it."

Taylor imitated and parodied the writings of various poets in Diversions of the Echo Club (London, 1873; Boston, 1876). In 1874 Taylor traveled to Iceland to report for the Tribune on the one thousandth anniversary of the first European settlement there.

During March 1878, the U.S. Senate confirmed his appointment as United States Minister to Prussia. Mark Twain, who traveled to Europe on the same ship, was envious of Taylor's command of German.

Taylor's travel writings were widely quoted by congressmen seeking to defend racial discrimination. For example, Richard Townshend (D-IL) quoted passages from Taylor such as "the Chinese are morally, the most debased people on the face of the earth," and "A Chinese city is the greatest of all abominations."

A few months after arriving in Berlin, Taylor died there on December 19, 1878. His body was returned to the U.S. and buried in Kennett Square, Pennsylvania. The New York Times published his obituary on its front page, referring to him as "a great traveler, both on land and paper". Shortly after his death, Henry Wadsworth Longfellow wrote a memorial poem in Taylor's memory, at the urging of Oliver Wendell Holmes, Sr.

Legacy and honors

Cedarcroft, Taylor's home from 1859 to 1874, which he built near Kennett Square, is preserved as a National Historic Landmark.

The Bayard Taylor School was added to the National Register of Historic Places in 1988.

The Bayard Taylor Memorial Library is in Kennett Square.

Evaluations

Though he wanted to be known most as a poet, Taylor was mostly recognized as a travel writer during his lifetime. Modern critics have generally accepted him as technically skilled in verse, but lacking imagination and, ultimately, consider his work as a conventional example of 19th-century sentimentalism.

His translation of Faust, however, was recognized for its scholarly skill and remained in print through 1969. According to the 1920 edition of Encyclopedia Americana:

> It is by his translation of Faust, one of the finest attempts of the kind in any literature, that Taylor is generally known; yet as an original poet he stands well up in the second rank of Americans. His Poems of the Orient and his Pennsylvania ballads comprise his best work. His verse is finished and sonorous, but at times over-rhetorical.

According to the 1911 edition of Encyclopædia Britannica:

Taylor's most ambitious productions in poetry—- his Masque of the Gods (Boston, 1872), Prince Deukalion; a lyrical drama (Boston, 1878), The Picture of St John (Boston, 1866), Lars; a Pastoral of Norway (Boston, 1873), and The Prophet; a tragedy (Boston, 1874)—- are marred by a ceaseless effort to overstrain his power. But he will be remembered by his poetic and excellent translation of Goethe's Faust (2 vols, Boston, 1870-71) in the original metres.

Taylor felt, in all truth, the torment and the ecstasy of verse; but, as a critical friend has written of him, his nature was so ardent, so full-blooded, that slight and common sensations intoxicated him, and he estimated their effect, and his power to transmit it to others, beyond the true value. He had, from the earliest period at which he began to compose, a distinct lyrical faculty: so keen indeed was his ear that he became too insistently haunted by the music of others, pre-eminently of Tennyson. But he had often a true and fine note of his own. His best short poems are The Metempsychosis of the Pine and the well-known Bedouin love-song.

In his critical essays Bayard Taylor had himself in no inconsiderable degree what he wrote of as that pure poetic insight which is the vital spirit of criticism. The most valuable of these prose dissertations are the Studies in German Literature (New York, 1879).

In Appletons' Cyclopædia of American Biography of 1889, Edmund Clarence Stedman gives the following critique:

His poetry is striking for qualities that appeal to the ear and eye, finished, sonorous in diction and rhythm, at times too rhetorical, but rich in sound, color, and metrical effects. His early models were Byron and Shelley, and his more ambitious lyrics and dramas exhibit the latter's peculiar, often vague, spirituality. Lars, somewhat after the manner of Tennyson, is his longest and most attractive narrative poem. Prince Deukalion was designed for a masterpiece; its blank verse and choric interludes are noble in spirit and mould. Some of Taylor's songs, oriental idyls, and the true and tender Pennsylvanian ballads, have passed into lasting favor, and show the native quality of his poetic gift. His fame rests securely upon his unequalled rendering of Faust in the original metres, of which the first and second parts appeared in 1870 and 1871. His commentary upon Part II for the first time interpreted the motive and allegory of that unique structure. (Source: Wikipedia)

CPSIA information can be obtained
at www.ICGtesting.com
Printed in the USA
BVHW031110290819
557144BV00006B/133/P